The NINTH NIGHT of HANUKKAH

by Erica S. Perl

illustrated by Shahar Kober

STERLING CHILDREN'S BOOKS
New York

On the **first night** of Hanukkah, Mom couldn't find the menorah.
"Special delivery!" said Dad, arriving with pizza.
Max and Rachel looked at each other.
No menorah? No latkes?

"It's just for tonight," said Mom. "I'm sure we'll find our Hanukkah things tomorrow."
Exhausted from unpacking, the family sat down to dinner in their new apartment.

It was nice . . . but it didn't
feel quite like Hanukkah.

On the **second night**, the missing menorah
still hadn't turned up.
"Should we go to the store?" asked Max.
"No, we'll find it soon," said Rachel. "Besides,
I have an idea for tonight."

Rachel made a beautiful menorah.
Max helped her decorate it.

But when it came time to light the candles,
Mom realized she packed them with the menorah.

"Now should we go to the store?" asked Max.
Mom checked her watch and shook her head.
"Everything's probably closed by now."

Max and Rachel convinced Mom to let them ask
one neighbor.

They knocked on 2C, right next door, and explained the situation to Mrs. Mendez.

"Would these work?"
she asked.

"Maybe," said Rachel.

Dad lit the **shamash**. Max and Rachel
each used it to light a candle.
Then Max and Rachel both got presents.

It was nice . . . but it didn't feel quite like Hanukkah.

On the **third night**, Dad offered to make latkes.
He just needed to find his lucky latke pan.
As Dad searched through box after box, Max
followed his nose downstairs . . .

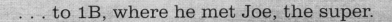

. . . to 1B, where he met Joe, the super.

"Welcome to the building," said Joe.
"Need anything? Let me know."
"Anything?" asked Max, eyeing the
steaming platter. Joe happily shared.

It was nice . . . but it didn't
feel quite like Hanukkah.

On the **fourth night**, Max said, "Let's play dreidel!"
One problem: no dreidel.
"I'm beginning to think one of our boxes got lost,"
said Dad.
So, Mom called the moving company.
And Max and Rachel set out to find a dreidel.

The Watson twins, who lived upstairs
in 3B, didn't have one.
But they did have a toy that could
spin and spin.

It was nice . . . but it didn't
feel quite like Hanukkah.

On the **fifth night**, Max and Rachel figured out a
way to play dreidel.

Which meant they needed gelt.

"No chocolate coins, but I do have these,"
said Mr. Patel, in 4A.

It was nice . . . but it didn't
feel quite like Hanukkah.

On the **sixth night**, Rachel wanted to have
a Hanukkah sing-along.
But Mom's guitar hadn't arrived yet.
"Gigi has one!" shouted the Watson twins,
running up to 5C.

It turned out they were **almost** right.

Mom taught Gigi the chords to "Rock of Ages," and everyone sang.

It was nice . . . but it didn't feel quite like Hanukkah.

On the seventh night, Max and Rachel discovered they were missing something else. "How do you wrap a present without wrapping paper?" On their way outside, they saw Dr. Lee reading in the lobby.

When they asked him where to buy wrapping
paper, he handed them the comics.
"Try using these," suggested Dr. Lee.
So, they did.

It was nice . . . but it **still** didn't
feel quite like Hanukkah.

On the **eighth night**, Max realized what their
Hanukkah needed: jelly donuts!
It took knocking on several doors, but finally Max
got his jelly.
From the twins' mom in 3B.

Just not in donut form.

"That was nice . . ." said Rachel, as they walked downstairs.

Max took a big bite and finished her thought:

"*Mmuht it mmuhsn't* feel quite like Hummukkuh."

The next morning, there was a knock at the door.
"Special delivery!"
Only this time, it wasn't Dad or pizza.
And it wasn't the long-lost box.

"Let's have a Hanukkah sing-along tonight," suggested Mom.

"Last night was the eighth night," Rachel reminded her.
"It won't be Hanukkah anymore."

"Maybe it should be,"
said Max, pointing.
"Nine candles, nine
nights."

Rachel's eyes lit up.
She whispered to
Max.

Max whispered back, and together they
developed a plan.
With a box of candles and a box of crayons,
they set it in motion.

That evening, Max and Rachel waited.

And waited.

"Maybe this isn't going to work," said Max.

"It'll work," said Rachel, sounding more confident than she felt.

Just then, there was a knock at the door.

And another. And another.

Max and Rachel thanked them all for coming.

Then they explained the reason for their
Shamash Night celebration.
"For eight nights of Hanukkah, the **shamash**
helps light all the other candles," said Max.
"Like all of you helped us," added Rachel. "So, we
wanted to say thanks—to the *shamash* and to you."
Just then, a voice called out from the back of the
line of guests.

"Special delivery!"

"The missing box!" said Mom.

"Now *that's* what I call a miracle!" said Dad.

In the box, Max and Rachel found
their family menorah,
Hanukkah candles,
Dad's lucky latke pan,
dreidels and gelt,
wrapping paper,
and Aunt Edith's recipe
for jelly donuts.

So, on the **ninth night** in their new home,
Max and Rachel and their new friends
talked and laughed,
ate and played games,
sang and danced by the light of many candles.

It was nice.
Really
REALLY
nice.
And best of all,
it felt *exactly*
like Hanukkah.

The Story of Hanukkah*

The story of Hanukkah happened a long, long time ago in the land of Israel. At that time, the Holy Temple in Jerusalem was the most special place for the Jewish people.

The Temple contained many beautiful objects, including a tall, golden menorah. Unlike menorahs of today, this one had seven (rather than nine) branches and was lit not by candles or light bulbs, but by oil. Every evening, oil would be poured into the cups that sat on top of the menorah. The Temple would glow with shimmering light.

At the time of the Hanukkah story, a cruel king named Antiochus ruled over the land of Israel. "I don't like the Jewish people," declared Antiochus. "They are so different from me. I don't celebrate Shabbat or read from the Torah, so why should they?" Antiochus ordered the Jewish people to stop being Jewish and to pray to Greek gods. "No more going to the Temple, no more celebrating Shabbat, and no more Torah!" shouted Antiochus. He sent his guards to ransack the Temple. They brought mud and garbage into the Temple. They broke furniture, tore curtains, and smashed the jars of oil that were used to light the menorah.

This made the Jews very angry. One Jew named Judah Maccabee cried out, "We must stop Antiochus! We must think of ways to make him leave the land of Israel." At first, Judah's followers, called the Maccabees, were afraid. "Judah," they said, "Antiochus has so many soldiers and they carry such big weapons. He even uses elephants to fight his battles. How can we Jews, who don't have weapons, fight against him?" Judah replied, "If we think very hard and plan very carefully, we will be able to defeat him." It took a long time, but at last the Maccabees chased Antiochus and his men out of Israel.

As soon as Antiochus and his soldiers were gone, the Jewish people hurried to Jerusalem to clean their Temple. What a mess! The beautiful menorah was gone, and the floor was covered with trash, broken furniture, and jagged pieces from the shattered jars of oil. The Maccabees built a new menorah. At first they worried that they would not be able to light their new menorah, but they searched and searched, until at last they found one tiny jar of oil—enough to light the menorah for just one evening. The Maccabees knew that it would be at least eight days until they could prepare more oil, but they lit the menorah anyway. To their surprise, this little jar of oil burned for eight days. The Jewish people could not believe their good fortune. First, their small army had chased away Antiochus's large army, and now the tiny jar of oil had lasted for eight whole days!

The Jewish people prayed and thanked God for these miracles. Every year during Hanukkah, Jews light menorahs for eight days to remember the miracles that happened long ago.

* The transliterated word *Hanukkah* can be spelled in a number of different ways—including *Chanukah, Chanuka*, etc.